Zombie Ed 101

The spit wad sailed from my straw and bounced off Bo Newt's skull with a satisfying *thwop!*

"Can I borrow your eraser?" I waved a hand before his face. But my classmate kept on staring like his choo-choo didn't go back to the station anymore.

"Science good," he slurred.

Uh-oh.

Something was definitely wrong. I'd seen students lobotomized by a boring science class before, but they usually snapped out of it after you hit them with a spit wad or gave them a double-strength noogie.

"Bo, you okay?" I whispered.

He put a finger to his lips. "*Shhh.* Teacher talking."

I frowned. Since when had Bo Newt ever cared about anything Mr. Ratnose had to say, except "Class dismissed"?

First, chatty Eena Moe went tongue-tied. Now, something had turned Bo the Brat into Percival Priss, Law-Abiding Student and All-Around Wuss.

One zombie is normal. But two zombies is strange, even for Emerson Hicky.

I smelled a mystery. And where mystery led, I followed.

Especially if it led away from science class.

The Big Nap

Chet Gecko Mysteries

The Chameleon Wore Chartreuse
The Mystery of Mr. Nice
Farewell, My Lunchbag
The Big Nap
The Hamster of the Baskervilles

And coming soon

This Gum for Hire
Trouble Is My Beeswax
The Malted Falcon
Give My Regrets to Broadway

The Big Nap

FROM THE TATTERED CASEBOOK OF

CHET GECKO
PRIVATE EYE

Bruce Hale

HARCOURT, INC.

Orlando • Austin • New York • San Diego • London

www.HarcourtBooks.com

First Harcourt paperbacks edition 2002
First published 2001

The Library of Congress has cataloged the
hardcover edition as follows:
Hale, Bruce.
The big nap: from the tattered casebook of
Chet Gecko, private eye/by Bruce Hale.
p. cm.
"A Chet Gecko mystery."
Summary: Someone is turning the students at Emerson
Hicky Elementary into zombies, and it's up to fourth-
grade private eye Chet Gecko to find out who.
[1. Geckos—Fiction. 2. Animals—Fiction.
3. Schools—Fiction. 4. Mystery and detective stories.]
I. Title.
PZ7.H1295Bi 2001
[Fic]—dc21 2001000844
ISBN 978-0-15-202521-2
ISBN 978-0-15-202479-6 pb

Text set in Bembo
Display type set in Elroy
Designed by Ivan Holmes

H J L N P Q O M K I

To my sisters, with much aloha

A private message from the private eye ...

Next to catching crooks, one of my favorite pastimes is catching z's. Have you ever noticed how the whole world looks rosier after a nap?

(That is, unless you wake up with graham crackers mushed into your face.)

The only thing I like better than a good snooze is a good meal. And the only thing I like better than a good meal is ... a nice, juicy mystery.

I love a mystery. Who am I? Chet Gecko, Private Eye—the best lizard detective at Emerson Hicky Elementary. It's not just my opinion. . . . Ask anybody.

My curiosity has gotten me into spots tighter than a hippo's tutu. No big deal; I'm still here. But one time, I cut things a little too close for comfort, and I almost found myself sleeping The Big Nap.

(That's the one where you never wake up for milk and cookies.)

My classmates were being hypnotized by some evil power (no, not math class—another evil power). And much as I might have wanted to hit the snooze button and let sleeping dogs lie, I couldn't afford forty winks.

The clock was ticking. If the sinister sandman caught up with me, it'd be sweet dreams for this private eye.

And that kind of beauty rest I don't need.

1

Chairman of the Bored

It was dumb of me, I know.

When you're a fourth grader, you don't take a shortcut across the sixth graders' playground. Not when they're playing on it.

It's safer to wear red undies and dance the hootchy-koo in front of a raging bull, or to dip a toe in a piranha's swimming pool.

But private eyes live dangerously. Besides, I was late for lunch.

Green and grumpy and ready to eat, I slipped along a line of krangleberry trees. Then I heard it.

Crink-crank-cronk!

Heavy footfalls crunched behind the next tree.

Something hefty—a T-rex, a grizzly, maybe Bigfoot?—was stalking me. I stopped short, and out popped Herman the Gila Monster.

I'd rather have met Bigfoot.

He leaned down into my face. "Hey, Gecko!" Herman's breath almost melted my hat. The guy never heard of mouthwash?

"What's up, Herman?" I said.

He stared at me with an expression that was about as cute as a bowlful of baby rattlesnakes. "This not fourth graders' playground. Beat it, Gecko— before I beat you."

"Still sore about those two months of detention?" I asked. "You should have thought of that before you tried to swipe the school mascot."

Herman wanted to make a snappy comeback. I could tell, because his forehead wrinkled with the effort and his jaw dropped open.

The silence stretched like your grandpa's oldest T-shirt.

"Don't strain yourself," I said, taking a moment to straighten my hat. A private eye stays cool under pressure. "Stick to one-syllable words."

The Gila monster pointed a shotgun-sized finger across the playground. "Go!" he growled.

"That'll do nicely." A private eye also knows when to split.

I turned, only to find the path blocked by a double scoop of ugly—Rocky Rhode and Erik Nidd, standing side by side.

Uh-oh.

I was doomed.

But that had never stopped me from wisecracking before.

"Sorry, ladies," I said. "I'm all full up on Girl Sprout cookies. Go peddle your wares somewheres else."

No response. Not even a "get lost" snarl. Only a quiet *beep-bop boop.*

I looked closer.

Both the horned toad and her tarantula pal had their eyes glued to handheld video games. And with a spider, that's a lot of eyes to glue.

I cleared my throat.

"Beat it," said Erik.

"We got better things to do than smush geckos," added Rocky.

Better things to do than beat me up? How rude. But then, how lucky.

Herman looked like he'd just been told the Wicked Witch of the West was actually an Avon lady. "Hey, you guyyys," he whined. "Get Gecko!"

I decided not to wait around until the big lug figured out he could mop the floor with me all by himself. "It's so hard to say good-bye," I said. "So let's just say *hasta la pasta*."

I slipped between Rocky and Erik, and hotfooted it for the cafeteria. They say discretion is the better part of valor; it's also better than a trip to the nurse's office.

After a while, I slowed to a brisk walk. Too much exercise can scramble the brains. And the only thing I like scrambled is my Eggs 'n' Termites à la Chet.

At the lunch counter, Mrs. Bagoong heaped my tray with scorpion stir-fry and lice foo yung. Wednesday is Asian-food day at Emerson Hicky cafeteria.

I scoped out the scene. Boring with a capital B. But I knew someone who might have a new mystery to crack.

Like at most lunchtimes, I parked my carcass beside my fine feathered partner, Natalie Attired. She was a whiz with puzzles and clues. Around school, her smart mouth had earned her a reputation as a black belt in tongue fu.

Just the kind of dame you want working your side of the street. We share a passion for mysteries, but I don't share her passion for worms.

Natalie's pretty sharp for a mockingbird—heck, pretty sharp for any kind of critter.

4

"Hey, Chet," she said, "what's an Eskimo's favorite food?" She looked at me wide-eyed. "Iceberg-ers! Get it?"

Well, maybe not *that* sharp.

I sighed.

She cackled and pecked at her stir-fry. "So what's the tale, nightingale? Any fresh mysteries to solve?"

I sighed again. "I was about to ask you. The mysteries in this school are about as fresh as Herman's armpits."

"That bad?" asked Natalie.

"Well, maybe not as stinky," I said.

We munched in silence for a while. If the detective biz got any slower, I'd have to mow lawns for candy money. And Chet Gecko is no lawn mower.

"Hey," said Natalie. "I know: That kid Popper is missing from school—maybe she's been kidnapped!"

I picked a scorpion stinger out of my stir-fry. "Nope. Home with the chicken pox. I checked."

"Hmmm..." Natalie pointed toward the lunch counter, where a huge possum in sunglasses was loading up his tray. "What about him? That guy looks mighty suspicious."

I glanced over. "I think he's the new librarian. Stop trying to cheer me up."

Natalie shrugged. "Suit yourself, señor."

I scanned the lunchroom. Nothing but food and foolishness. Bo Newt was giving an atomic wedgie to some kid in the corner. Another classmate, Waldo the furball, was stupefying three second graders with his magic tricks.

I looked the other way. Two mice practiced their karate moves on a tabletop. No mysteries there.

In fact, nothing shaking but the Jell-O on the trays.

"I just wish something would happen," I said. "Anything. I'm so bored, I'm baiting sixth graders for fun."

I didn't know it, but before another day passed, I'd have to eat my words. And they wouldn't be as tasty as the doodlebug pudding.

But then, not much is.

2

Trouble Is My Beeswax

After lunch, I dragged my tail out onto the playground. Natalie followed. A pack of rats played King of the Hill on a jungle gym. One of them shoved his last rival aside and stood alone on the top.

"Rat king—now there's a great job," I said. "Looks like it's livelier than detective work."

Natalie practiced ignoring me.

A knot of kids had gathered near a broad oak tree. We walked closer. Over a ring of shoulders, I glimpsed their entertainment: A bully circling his prey.

No mystery there, either. Just the everyday law of the playground jungle.

From what I could see, the bully was a beefy muskrat named Fred-o. This fifth-grade Attila the

Hun could squeeze lunch money from a victim quicker than foul wind from a hop-toad's heinie. I figured his victim was a goner.

But by the time we arrived, the group was breaking up. Fred-o grinned at his prey, a skinny stoat (or weasel—I can't tell them apart).

"Gee, thanks," said Fred-o. He patted the little guy's shoulder and trundled off.

The weasel (or stoat) smoothed his whiskers and strolled the opposite way.

He looked familiar.

"Isn't that the new kid in your class?" Natalie asked. "Sammy something?"

"Oh yeah, that's him."

It made sense. New kids were usually bully bait. But this one seemed to have something on the ball.

He eased across the grass like syrup on a pancake, with a cut in his strut and a glide in his stride. I wished I felt half as chipper.

Natalie and I flopped down under the scrofulous tree, my favorite thinking spot. She cleaned her feathers while I thought long thoughts—mostly about how to buy my afternoon snack. My wallet was as empty as a newborn kitten's threat.

My eyes hadn't been closed for more than three seconds when I heard a small sound like a seasick gopher.

Heh-hyewm.

Eyes shut, I said, "I didn't know mockingbirds got hair balls."

The sound repeated itself. *Heh-hyewm.*

I looked up.

There she stood, a thick slab of nothing special: A plump guinea pig in a pearly pink sweater. Her eyes glistened like big brown pools of chocolate sauce. She twisted the strap on her book bag.

"If you're gonna ralph, sister," I said, "use the bushes."

The guinea pig's lips clamped down until her mouth was as tight as the PTA's purse. "I was clearing my throat," she said primly. She plucked an invisible speck of lint from her sleeve. "I'm looking for a gecko named Chet."

I told her that I was a gecko named Chet. And that my partner was a mockingbird named Natalie. But for the right money, we'd be a Ukrainian bug-juggling act named Sturm and Drang.

The guinea pig nodded her head slightly. "You may call me Meena Moe."

It seemed only fair. That was her name.

"Okay, Meena Moe," I said. "Hey, you don't happen to have two sisters named Eena and Minah, do you?"

She caught her breath. "How did you know?"

"Lucky guess." I rubbed my chin and looked up at her. "So, what's the scam, ma'am?"

Meena gave me a quick once-over and toyed with her book bag some more. "What's a guy like you charge?" she asked.

"Why's a dame like you want to know?"

"I've got trouble."

"Don't we all," I said. "What's yours?"

"My youngest sister, Eena. Lately, she's been acting strangely."

"Maybe it's gas," said Natalie. She grinned.

Meena frowned. "Not likely. She's—well, she used to be so bright and chatty and chipper, and now she's a . . . she's a zombie."

Natalie and I exchanged glances. A case at last! And a supernatural one, to boot.

"What kind of zombie?" I asked Meena. "A flesh-eating, undead, graveyard-robbing, walks-in-the-night kind of zombie?"

Her eyes flashed. "Certainly not!" she said. "Mother would never allow it. No, Eena just stares blankly and speaks in short sentences. Her vocabulary has deteriorated dreadfully—like she's been lobotomized!"

"Sounds like too much late-night TV to me," I said.

Meena sniffed. "*Hmph!* I know my sister. Something's wrong, and I'd like you to find out what it is." She fished in her book bag. "How about fifty cents a day, plus expenses?"

I gave her my tough-guy smirk. "How about seventy-five cents a day, and fifty cents now, as a retainer?"

Meena squinched up her nose, calculating. Finally, she nodded.

I might not have liked her prissiness, but I liked her money okay. A gecko's gotta eat.

I dropped the coins into my pocket. "Now, where can we find the charming Miss Eena?"

"She's two years younger than me; so at present, she's a third grader. You'll find her in Ms. Glick's class." Meena turned and minced off. "Ta-ta. Keep me apprised of your progress."

I frowned. *"Apprised?"*

Natalie made a face. "Ms. *Glick*?"

Ms. Glick was known around school as the Beast of Room 3. We were really going to earn our fee this time.

The Beast could nurse a grudge long enough for it to have baby grudges of its own. She was not a card-carrying member of the Chet Gecko Fan Club.

But in spite of everything, I smiled. We had a case at last!

Oh, silly me.

3

Gator Aided

Natalie and I sidled up to Ms. Glick's classroom. I tried the door. Locked. Her class was still at lunch or playing carefree third-grade games. I scoped out the empty hall.

Now, where would a guinea pig zombie go for fun?

"Natalie, what do you know about zombies?"

"Not much," she said. "But I know which zombie ate too much porridge."

"Eh? Who's that?"

Natalie's eyes twinkled. "*Ghoul*dilocks!" she cackled.

I shook my head. Sometimes, having a mockingbird partner can be a pain.

Natalie looked past my shoulder and stiffened.

"That's it, Natalie. To think like a zombie, act like a zombie."

"Well, well, what a pleasure," rasped a voice smooth as a gravel-and-chain-saw milk shake.

Ms. Glick!

Toe by toe, I peeled myself off the wall I'd jumped onto. Those quick gecko reflexes again. I climbed down and straightened my hat.

"Trying to get a head start on your next detention session, Mr. Gecko?" sneered the Beast of Room 3. A frown split her thick alligator snout.

I squinted up at her, pasting a counterfeit smile on my kisser. "Ah, Ms. Glick. When I'm away from you, the minutes pass like hours. I was just telling Natalie about the good ol' days in your classroom, when—"

"Do I look like a dinner roll to you?" she asked.

"Uh, no," I said.

"Then stop trying to butter me up," snarled Ms. Glick. "What do you want?"

Enough charm. "I'm on a case," I said.

"Mister, you *are* a case."

I let that one slide. "It involves one of your students," I said. "Eena Moe."

Ms. Glick unlocked her door. She smiled back at us over a broad, scaly shoulder, her pearly choppers twinkling in the sunshine. "Come inside," she said.

Natalie gulped. We followed Ms. Glick. I glanced around at my old third-grade classroom. Booger-green walls, rusty heating vents, battered desks—ah, how the memories came rushing back.

Of course, they didn't have far to rush. One week earlier, I'd been in that same room for detention.

As Ms. Glick settled her bulk at the desk, I asked, "Have you noticed anything different about Eena lately?"

"And why should I tell you if I had?" she growled.

"Because of my winning personality?" I said.

"Hah!" She snorted.

I frowned at Natalie. We should've known Ms. Glick would play hardball. I drew myself up and squared my shoulders.

"Okay, fine," I said. "Don't help us. But just know, when poor, sad Eena goes down the drain like a soggy hankie—"

"You don't know what you're talking about," said the Beast. "Eena's a pip."

"A pip?" said Natalie, cocking her head.

"A peach, a sweetheart, a good egg," said Ms. Glick. "In fact, she's even nicer than usual, if possible."

"Huh?" I said. I'm a smooth interviewer. Sometimes.

"You want me to spell it out for you, detective boy?" said the Beast. "Okay. Eena doesn't gossip in class anymore. Eena cleans the erasers. Eena pays attention—unlike you, Chester."

I hate it when they use my full name. "So... she's not a zombie?"

"*Zombie?!* Double *hah!*" Ms. Glick waved a leathery arm at the empty classroom. "Mister, if she's a zombie, I'd like a whole class of them!"

She chuckled. It sounded like a cave full of hungry werewolves converging on a meatball pizza.

"Now, buzz off!" snarled Ms. Glick.

We could take a hint. Natalie and I beat feet. Farther down the hall, we stopped to regroup.

"What do you make of that?" I asked.

"I don't know," said Natalie. "Those guinea pigs are a little squirrelly, if you ask me. Maybe Meena's imagining things."

I wasn't imagining Meena's cool quarters. I jingled the change in my pocket.

"She's the client," I said, "and she knows her sister. Let's humor her."

Still, as I watched Natalie head for her classroom, I wondered if this zombie business would turn out to be just another soggy firecracker—more fizzle than sizzle.

But then again, what did I have on my plate that was more important than this case? Studying?

The lunch bell cut short my laugh.

I sighed and went to class.

4

Science Friction

If classrooms were drugstore products, Mr. Rat-nose's class would be SnorMore, the cure for insomnia.

Right and left of me, heads and eyelids drooped like spaghetti from yesterday's food fight. Shirley Chameleon slumbered behind her book. Waldo the furball looked like he was hibernating.

And then Mr. Ratnose ratcheted up the snooze factor. "It's science time, boys and girls!"

Scattered groans greeted his remark.

"Geology is the study of the Earth and its history," he said. "Now, who can tell us what the Earth is made of?"

My attention wandered like a disobedient dog.

On a piece of notebook paper, I doodled a couple of aliens dissecting the planet. They had strapped it to an operating table and were slicing open the Earth like a ripe melon.

Maybe they'd do the same to my head and put me out of my misery.

I started to erase an alien's face, when—*kzztch!*—the last of my eraser wore down. The page tore.

Then an even worse sound hit my ears.

"Oh, Chet?"

It was my teacher. He held up a pointy rock in his hand like the Holy Lump of Saint Hasenpfeffer. "Can you tell us what kind of rock this is?" he asked.

"Rocks are rocks," I said. "I take 'em for granite."

Mr. Ratnose's lip curled in a sneer. "Not even close. Can anyone else tell us?"

Bitty Chu, the gopher, flagged her arm in the traditional oh-oh-oh-call-on-me signal.

My eyes drifted back to my drawing. *Drat!* I needed a new eraser to improve my latest masterpiece. Who would have one?

I looked around. There he was, right before me: Bo Newt, the sassy salamander—your fourth-grade source for rubber-band guns, whoopee cushions, squirting flowers, art supplies, and other trouble-making tools.

I hissed at him, "Bo! Lend me your eraser."

Nothing. He watched Mr. Ratnose closely. The back of Bo's thick head gleamed slightly, like a fridge in the moonlight.

Stronger measures were needed.

The spit wad sailed from my straw and bounced off Bo Newt's skull with a satisfying *thwop!*

"Duhhh." Bo turned to me with a loose grin. His eyes were as empty as a bully's mailbox on Valentine's Day.

"I said, can I borrow your eraser?" I waved a hand before his face. But my classmate kept on staring like his choo-choo didn't go back to the station anymore.

"Science good," he slurred.

Uh-oh.

Something was definitely wrong. I'd seen students lobotomized by a boring science class before, but they usually snapped out of it after you hit them with a spit wad or gave them a double-strength noogie.

At last, Bo handed me his eraser. His wide-open mouth could've caught a freight load of flies, if he'd known how to shut it. Bo had never been the sharpest crayon in the pack, but this was ridiculous.

"Bo, you okay?" I whispered.

He put a finger to his lips. "*Shhh.* Teacher talking."

I frowned. Since when had Bo Newt ever cared

about anything Mr. Ratnose had to say, except "Class dismissed"?

"Heh, heh, heh." A quiet snicker drifted over from the next row. The new kid, that skinny weasel from the playground, waggled his eyebrows at me and imitated Bo's blank face.

Bo didn't even notice. He turned back to catch Mr. Ratnose's geology lecture, which was zipping along like a glacier with arthritis.

"He's as clueless as a porcupine at a polka lesson," Sammy whispered.

It was pretty rude. I had to admit, though, I liked the way he put things. It reminded me of someone.

But I couldn't stop to think who; my detective instincts had kicked in.

First, chatty Eena Moe went tongue-tied. Now, something had turned Bo the Brat into Percival Priss, Law-Abiding Student and All-Around Wuss.

One zombie is normal. But two zombies is strange, even for Emerson Hicky.

I smelled a mystery. And where mystery led, I followed.

Especially if it led away from science class.

5

Little Bo, Creep

At recess, I waited outside the classroom for Bo Newt. And waited. And waited.

Finally, after all the other kids had split, I poked my head through the door. What I saw left me colder than a penguin's lunch box.

A blackboard. A student. Bo was cleaning the blackboard! I blinked, then shook my head. Usually the teacher's pets—Igor Beaver, Bitty Chu, and Cassandra the Stool Pigeon—fought for the honor of erasing.

But Bo?

My salamander buddy liked to roughhouse, tell booger jokes, and draw rude pictures. He had about as much class as a wildebeest in a dinner jacket. Bo was no teacher's pet.

Things were worse than I'd thought.

At last, Bo finished erasing and exited the class-room with an armload of books.

I fell in beside him. "Hey, ace, what's shaking?"

He stared straight ahead, shuffling like a windup toy.

"Saw you at the blackboard," I said. "You haven't gone all teacher's pet on me, have you?"

This was a serious insult. The old Bo Newt would've decked me in a heartbeat.

This new Bo turned his head toward me stiffly. "Bo help teacher. Teacher good."

I grabbed his arm. "Okay, Bo. The gag's gone far enough. Nobody's laughing."

He slipped from my grasp and shambled off. "Bye-bye. Must study."

I blinked. Bo wasn't that good an actor. I knew; I'd been in a play with him. That meant that my classmate had had a serious personality trans-plant.

Or maybe he was a real zombie.

I watched the slow-moving salamander approach the library. He reached the door at the same time as a guinea pig in a yellow sweater.

Eena? She looked like a shorter clone of her sister, but she moved like Bo, in a stiff-legged trance.

They bowed to each other, he held the door for her, and they went inside.

It seemed Emerson Hicky was having an epidemic of good manners.

Stranger and stranger.

I spotted the new kid, Sammy, just down the hall, chatting with Fred-o the bully. Sammy passed a bag to the big muskrat, who chuckled and sauntered off.

When Sammy noticed me, he waved me over. I strolled up to him.

"Heya, pal," he said in a voice smooth as creamy peanut butter. "Sammy's the name, weaseling's the game."

"I'm—" I started to say.

He held up a paw. "Hey, I know who you are, Chet Gecko. You're a big lizard on campus—the man with the plan."

It was flattery, I admit. But when a guy's right, he's right.

I checked out Sammy. He lounged against a pole, cooler than a root beer Popsicle. His brown fur was glossy, and he had that knowing look in his eyes, like the fifth graders who practice kissing behind the bungalows.

"You new here?" I asked.

"Just fell off the turnip truck," he said. "We move around a lot, so I'm always the new kid." Sammy

chuckled. "It's about as much fun as a long ride on a busted roller coaster, but I'm used to it."

I liked his plucky attitude and the way he talked.

"Made many friends yet?" I asked.

Sammy shrugged. "A few. I'm still sorting out the cool kids from the jerks."

"Yeah? Better do some more sorting. That Fred-o is bad news on webbed feet."

Sammy waved off my comment. "Don't worry, I can handle that goombah."

"Okay," I said, "it's your lunch money."

The weasel snapped his fingers. "Say, listen: My mom's a good cook. You wanna come over for dinner some night?"

Dinner? One of my favorite words.

"Yeah, sure," I said. "That'd be fine."

He flashed a smile. "Cool," he said. "Well, plant you now..."

"...And dig you later," I finished.

Sammy flowed off down the hall like a length of brown silk tied to a king snake's tail.

I saw a familiar figure across the library lawn. Natalie flapped up as I crossed to meet her.

"Where you been?" she said.

"Having a chat with the new kid, Sammy."

She watched him glide around the corner. "I don't like him. He seems sneaky."

"Naw," I said. "He's all right. I'm gonna go over and have dinner at his house sometime."

"Uh-huh." She raised an eyebrow. "Now, can we park the welcome wagon and get back to our case?"

"You bet."

As we headed for the swings, I filled her in on Bo's odd behavior.

"*Two* zombies?" she said.

"Yup. They may be connected, but let's concentrate on the one we're getting paid for."

"Okeydokey. We'll take things one zombie at a time."

We sat on the swings. We swung. A horsefly circled above us, and I zapped him with my tongue—*thwick!* Fuel food for detective work.

But before we could do any serious thinking, the bell rang. Rats. It's hard to make progress on a case when bells keep ringing like Santa's sleigh in a cyclone.

I hopped off the swing. We trudged back to class.

"Let's try to get close to Eena; see what we can pick up," I said.

"Whatever it is, I hope it's not catching."

"Ha, ha. Meet me outside her room after school."

"It's a deal, McNeal," she said. Natalie hurried to her class.

I stopped by the candy machine and spent most

of Meena's retainer fee on a Pillbug Crunch bar. For my own reasons, I hoped the case would take a couple of days to solve.

There's nothing more selfish than a PI with a sweet tooth.

6

Danger in the Dewey Decimal System

Soon as the last bell chimed, I slid out the door like a wombat on ice. We had to catch up with Eena before she got too far.

I needn't have worried.

As Natalie and I met by Room 3, I sneaked a peek inside, past the steady stream of departing kids. Eena was cleaning blackboards for Ms. Glick.

Such a polite zombie. Maybe she could tackle my messy bedroom next.

Natalie and I slipped out of sight, just around the corner. Ms. Glick had kid radar, and it wouldn't pay to get caught in her sights.

We leaned against the wall, and Natalie whistled a little tune.

"What's that you're singing?" I asked.

"'The Mock-arena.'"

"Yeah? Well you'll be singing 'Bye Bye Birdie' if you don't knock it off. We're supposed to be spying."

Natalie put a wing feather to my mouth. "*Shhh.* Here she comes."

We faded back behind some scraggly bushes and watched as Eena shuffled by. But we didn't need to hide. She wouldn't have noticed anything short of a flying saucer crash-landing on her foot, spitting out a string of aliens singing, "Scoobie-doobie-doo."

Still, it never hurts to be sly. Natalie and I slipped out of the bushes and idled down the hall behind the yellow-sweatered guinea pig.

Eena didn't look left or right. She marched, slow as the last minute of the last day of school. Up the hall, then right. Down another hall, then into . . . the library.

"Odd," I said to Natalie. "She went there at recess, too."

"Maybe she's got to study for her Monster Ed classes."

"Or maybe," I said, "something's going on in that library—something even scarier than required reading."

Natalie shrugged. "Dunno. But we need to go in there, anyway."

"Why's that?"

"Neither of us knows anything about zombies. What better place to find out than the library?"

She had a point. (Other than the one at the end of her beak, I mean.) After giving it a minute, we pushed through the library doors and into the cool quiet.

I scanned the book stacks. No Eena.

We poked into the computer room. Two bratty prairie dogs played video games free from the librarian's gaze, but still no Eena.

Hmm.

"She'll turn up," said Natalie. "Meantime, let's research."

She plunked her tail feathers into a seat and booted up an open computer. Within minutes, Natalie had collected a host of zombie Web sites: *The Undead & You, Harry's Happy Zombie Page, Hypnosis and Zombiism, Flesh-Eaters' Funtime, www.evilzombie.com*—and scads of others.

For some reason, I felt restless. "You check 'em out," I said. "I'll take another look around."

I reentered the main room, pacing up and down the deserted stacks. Where was the librarian?

Back behind his desk, I slipped into a short corridor lined with three doors. (Yeah, I know it's off-limits. So sue me; I'm a snoopy detective.)

One door led to the bathroom. Empty.

One door led to the storage room. Locked.

A faint murmur drifted through the third door, like a radio station beaming from Mars. I leaned closer. Some kind of meeting...?

I didn't hear him approach, but my nostrils flared at the smell. Eau de Roadkill, with just a hint of incense.

Now, who at Emerson Hicky was tough enough to wear that scent? I had to find out.

"Hidey-ho," rumbled a deep voice. "I'm the new librarian."

I turned. "Thanks, pal. You just saved me a lot of detective work."

My eyes met a fuzzy belly button. I craned my neck and looked up, up, up.

His hairy chest was no broader than the back end of a Mack truck, and he wasn't quite as tall as a redwood tree, but you could still tell: This was one big possum. Sleepy eyes lurked behind wraparound shades, and a blue beret crowned the whole affair.

Pretty snappy for a marsupial.

"Don't b'leeve I've had the pleasure," he said. "My handle is Aloyicious Theonlyest Bunk—but you can call me Cool Beans. May I...help you with somethin'?"

Caught red-handed while snooping, I improvised. "Um...yeah. I was just looking for some books on zombies. Nobody was around, so I..."

The big possum grinned, exposing two rows of sharp teeth. "Copacetic, daddy-o. Right this way."

He plopped a python-sized arm across my shoulders and steered me back to the book stacks. "You're in luck, little lizard. You're shootin' the breeze with the local expert on zombies, duppies, ghouls, spirits, and mocha lattes."

Cool Beans leaned down and plucked a book from the shelf. "And it's a swingin' thing you met me," he continued, "'cause this is the only book on zombies we got."

I glanced at the cover. *The Little Zombie That Could*. Not exactly the finest in ghoulish reference materials.

"So, Mr. ... uh, Beans," I said.

"Cool Beans," said the possum. "*Mister* is for squares and squirrels."

I nodded. "Cool Beans. I need to know how to tell if someone's gone zomboid. I mean, what are the signs?"

The burly possum narrowed his eyes. "Why you askin'?"

"Uh, it's for my class project," I said.

"Hmm," he said. "Well, your basic zombie stares straight ahead ... walks all stiff-legged ... talks zombie talk ..."

"Zombie talk?"

"Yeah, you know, like: 'Books good; modern art bad.' Stuff like that. Also, zombies follow orders like I follow the smell of fine espresso. You dig?"

I leaned against a chair back. "And how do you make a zombie?" I asked.

"Well, you—" Cool Beans glanced at the wall clock. "Oh, man, check out the time. I gotta split."

He headed for the hall behind his desk at a steady amble, which for a possum is like sprinting a fifty-yard dash. "Later, freighter," he said. "It's been uptown, way-out, and wild."

Cool Beans disappeared into the short corridor. A door opened and closed.

Curiouser and curiouser.

From what the big possum had said, both Bo Newt and Eena Moe had all the signs of advanced zombitude. I didn't know how they'd gotten that way. But I knew one thing.

For a simple librarian, this guy knew an awful lot about zombies—the kind of stuff you can't learn from books. Just ghost to show you: There's no ghoul like an old ghoul.

7

Home, Home, and Deranged

The library didn't feel so safe anymore. I dragged Natalie off the computer, and we headed for my place to regroup. My sharp detective mind needed some more fuel food.

Along the way, I filled Natalie in on my encounter with the new librarian and the mysterious sounds behind the closed door. We tried to guess what was happening in the library meeting room.

"Do you think Cool Beans is making zombies back there?" I asked.

"And they're what, shelving his books for him?" she said. "I dunno."

"Whatever it is, he wants to keep it under wraps."

We strolled down the sidewalk under heavy skies.

The clouds looked as gray as a rhino's rump at twilight and as full of rain as an overstuffed water balloon.

Natalie ran down her research results. "Man, there's a lot of info out there," she said. "Do you know, I even learned how to make a zombie float?"

"How do you make a zombie float?" I asked.

"A glass of root beer and two scoops of zombie!" Natalie squawked. "You sure stepped into that one."

I took a deep breath. A private eye stays calm, even in the face of extreme aggravation. "Did you pick up anything other than the latest zombie jokes?"

Natalie hopped off the curb and we crossed the street toward my house. "Absolutely. I learned that most zombies have had their souls sucked out of their bodies."

"Eeew," we said together. "Soul suckers."

"They can either be dead folks brought back to life, or living ones who get turned into slaves," Natalie said.

"And how do you enslave someone?"

She raised an eyebrow. "I was just reading that part when somebody dragged me off the computer."

I examined my fingerpads closely. "Is that so?"

"But," she said, "hypnosis is one way—that much I know."

We strolled into my backyard. By this time, my

little sister, Pinky, should've been all over me like brown on a chocolate bar. I looked around. No sign of her.

"*Shhh,*" I said. "Let's sneak into my office."

We tiptoed toward the clump of bamboo. My office sat just behind it, cleverly disguised as an old refrigerator box.

Beep-bop boop, came a sound from just ahead.

Either extraterrestrials were phoning home from my office or someone was playing a video game behind the bamboo.

"Pinky!" I said.

She didn't even look up from her handheld game. "Hmm?"

"Pinky, get back in the house." As the firstborn gecko, I had bossing-around privileges. And I never hesitated to use them.

"Mmkay," she said. Pinky rose obediently and walked up to the back door, still playing her game.

"Wow. That was easy," I said. "We should give her video games more often."

Natalie and I entered the office and broke into my stash of sugar-coated cockroach eggs. *Mmm,* life is sweet. I was ready for action.

"Okay, what do we know? One, Eena is acting like a zombie."

"Two, so is Bo Newt," said Natalie.

"Three, somebody or something enslaved them—maybe a hypnotist."

Natalie scratched herself with a claw. "Four, Bo and Eena spend lots of time at the library, where the zombie expert works."

"And five...," I said. "Do we have a five?"

Natalie shook her head.

I paced while Natalie fluffed her feathers. We needed a plan, a plot, a course of action. What we had was more questions than a six-page math test.

Natalie looked up. "What's our next step, O prince of detectives?"

"Um...I guess we try talking to Eena."

"We try talking to Eena?"

"Gee," I said. "You took the words right out of my mouth. And my tongue didn't feel a thing."

We decided to catch Eena the next morning, before class. Sometimes you can learn more if you grill someone in person (or in pig, as the case may be). If we played it right, maybe we could figure out how to get Meena's little sister out of her pickle.

If we played it wrong—well, no big deal. I wasn't in a hurry. I thought we had plenty of time.

I turned out to be wronger than a stuttering sidewinder at a spelling bee.

8

Ghoul of My Dreams

Next morning, the sun was chirping and the birds were shining. Or something like that. My sleep-starved brain was so groggy, it was hard to figure out which end to put the Cheerios in.

I dragged my sleepy self to Room 3. I didn't go inside, of course. I wasn't that sleepy. Facing a grumpy alligator first thing in the A.M. isn't my way to say "Good day, sunshine."

Instead, Natalie and I leaned against the wall outside, watching for a certain young zombie. We didn't have long to wait.

Shoof, shoof, shoof.

Eena shuffled down the hall like a rundown robot in a second-rate sci-fi movie. Of course, zombies always walk like that. (This I knew from watching lots of second-rate sci-fi.)

We eased off the wall and into her path. "Hi, Eena," I said. "We'd like a word with you."

Her dull eyes barely saw us. "Must go," she said. "Help teacher."

"This won't take a minute," I said. "We just want to chat." I steered her gently off to the side.

"Eena," said Natalie, "do you feel okay?"

"Feel fine," said Eena.

"Your sister is worried about you," I said.

"Feel fine," Eena repeated. "Must go."

This wasn't going to be as easy as I'd thought. Eena seemed like a graduate of the Frankenstein's

Monster School of Speechmaking. We'd be lucky to get more than three words at a time from her.

"Why do you have to go?" I asked.

"Must help teacher. Teacher good."

She tried to walk away. I grabbed her shoulder.

"You didn't help the teacher before, did you?" asked Natalie. "Why did you start?"

The questions confused Eena. Her empty eyes moved in slow circles, like a lost bumblebee in the bottom of a glass. It was kind of spooky.

"Be good, get allowance," she said. "Must go."

The guinea pig pushed past me and plodded into her classroom. I drew Natalie down the hall.

"'Be good, get allowance'?" I said. "What's this, a money zombie? I thought they only haunted Wall Street."

Natalie smirked. "Maybe she's only a part-dime ghoul, eh? That makes cents."

I groaned and led us to the cafeteria. A stray muffin might wipe out the taste of Natalie's puns.

We leaned through the kitchen door. Mrs. Bagoong, head cafeteria lady, was sliding a tray into her oven. Before I could even ask, she said, "Too early, Chet, honey. Come back in ten minutes."

Timing is everything.

I turned to go, but something caught my eye.

Deeper in the cafeteria, Shirley Chameleon leaned

against a table, playing some kind of game. Beyond her, a couple of salamanders were sitting on the bench nearest the stage, watching a top-hatted Waldo the furball. (We never could figure out what kind of animal he was.)

A hand-lettered sign on the stage read, THE GRATE WALDINI.

Natalie and I stepped closer.

"Obserrrve the watch in my hannnd," droned Waldo. "Baaack and forth, baaack and forth. You're getting sleeepy ..."

Natalie nudged me. "A hypnotist!" she whispered.

"What?" I said. "You don't think that Waldo ...?" I chuckled. "Waldo couldn't hypnotize anyone. His magic is so lame, he couldn't put his foot to sleep if he sat on it."

But while we watched, the salamanders grew slack-jawed.

"Raaaise your right haaand," said Waldo.

Both of the kids raised their left hands.

"Yooour other riiight," said Waldo.

They obeyed. I looked closer at my classmate, the doofus in the top hat. I'd always thought of Waldo as just a garden-variety nerd. Did he really have the hypnotic power to make a zombie?

Or was he so clueless he couldn't make toast without an instruction manual?

9

Wall-to-Wall Waldo

Recess came not a minute too soon. I was itching for action like a warthog in poison-ivy pants.

First things first. Time to grill Waldo like a bug on a porch light.

I beat him out the door and waited down the hall.

At recess, Waldo usually liked to practice his dorky magic tricks down by the playground. But not today. He was going to spill the beans first, and no disappearing act could save him.

Waldo slouched down the hall with his big bag o' magic.

"Waldo!" I said. "Just the furball I wanted to see."

"*Hur, hur.* You want me?" he said.

The bell rang. We had to get to class. But I was definitely going to keep an eye on that furball.

Math class—what a way to start the day. If you ask me, it's a close second to bamboo shoots under the fingernails.

But my teacher, Mr. Ratnose, wouldn't agree. He stood before the class, burbling like a kindergartner who's brought his booger collection for show-and-tell.

"Okay, class, listen carefully," he said. "A man gave one son ten cents and another son fifteen cents. What time is it?"

Math is one mystery I don't care if I ever solve. I looked around—slowly, so I wouldn't draw the teacher's attention. I had expected Snooze City, but instead, most of my classmates were watching Mr. Ratnose like he was their favorite TV show.

"Shirley Chameleon?" he asked.

"Math good," she slurred.

"Uh, yes," said Mr. Ratnose, "it is. Anyone else?"

A paw shot up. "Let's see, ten plus fifteen is twenty-five cents...the man gave a quarter to two...so the time is one forty-five!"

I glanced over. It was Igor Beaver, professional teacher's pet. He and Mr. Ratnose chuckled together.

A math joke—yuck.

Our teacher addressed the rest of us. "Get it?" he said. "One forty-five . . . a quarter to two?"

Deafening silence. Sammy the weasel smirked at me. Waldo frowned and fiddled with his pencil.

Mr. Ratnose's smile slipped from his face, bounced off the desk, and hit the floor, bruising itself badly.

"Open your geometry books," he snarled. "Let's get down to business."

As he prattled on about polygons, I eyeballed the class again. Many faces wore the same goofy stare as Bo Newt's. Math class could drive anyone around the bend.

But if my hunch was right, more than boredom was at work here. Someone sinister was enslaving my classmates.

Yesterday, I saw only a couple of stiffs, but today we had enough to cast a musical remake of *Flesh-Eaters over Broadway.*

This case was bigger than Eena's problem. It was time to get off the dime.

I had to figure out who was behind the zombie epidemic before Mr. X figured out I was after him.

Or else this private eye would end up in a chorus line, dancing the zombie mambo.

I hooked an arm through his and led Waldo alongside the building.

"Oh," he said, "you wanna watch my tricks?"

I sneered. "No, mister, I've had enough of your tricks."

"What do you mean?"

"It's time to come clean...Mr. Hypnotist."

Under heavy bangs, Waldo's eyes darted left and right, like frightened rabbits in a thicket. "I-I don't know what you're talking about," he said.

I crowded him against the wall. "Someone's been turning students into zombies around here—someone who knows hypnosis."

Waldo gulped. "Wasn't me," he said.

"Oh, no? How many hypnotists do you know at Emerson Hicky?"

I stared him down, eyeball to eyeball.

Waldo cracked like a mug you make your mom in art class. "O-okay! I *have* been practicing hypnosis. But not to hurt anybody."

"Tell it to the judge," I said. "You turned half our class into drooling zombies. And that poor little Eena—how could you?"

"Eena?"

My tail curled and snapped like a bullwhip. "You're dealing with powers you cannot comprehend. You've messed with the supernatural, buddy-boy, and now it's time to pay the piper."

Waldo hung his head, cowed. "I-I'm so-so sorry," he stammered. "I just wa-wanted to be in the school talent show!" He looked up. "But w-what piper? And who's Eena?"

"Oh, you know," I said, pacing before him. "That little third-grade guinea pig? One of your first victims, no doubt."

Waldo's face squinched up in puzzlement. "Wait—I didn't hypnotize any guinea pigs."

I stopped. "You didn't?"

"No," he said. "And I only tried hypnosis a few times." Waldo sighed. "Usually, they'd sing instead of dance, or pick their pocket instead of their nose..."

I gave him my best steely-eyed gaze. "Do you swear by the Golden Gopher?" (It's our school mascot. I think the gopher is kinda lame, but most of the fur-bearing students love it.)

"I swear by the Gopher," said Waldo. "I'm no hypnotist—I'm not even a very good magician. But I can do card tricks..." He rummaged in his bag.

I grabbed his arm. "No, that's okay. I believe you."

And I did. Waldo was about as good at lying as I was at skipping dessert. You could read his face like a book—the kind with very big letters and lots of pictures.

"Thanks for believing me," he said. "Now, what's this about zombies?"

I told Waldo what Natalie and I had learned so far. He might be a doofus, but no reason he had to turn into a zombie doofus.

"So keep an eye out," I said. "And if you see anything shady, let me know."

"You mean, like an oak tree? *Hur, hur.*"

I winced.

"Will do, Chet!" Waldo saluted clumsily. "Hey, you sure you don't wanna see me pull a scarf out of my—"

But before he could finish, I scooted off to find Natalie. Fun's fun, but a whole recess with Waldo would be too-too weird for words.

My partner waited in line at the tetherball court. A gangly crane was up. He swung at the ball and staggered off balance. The ball on its leash whipped around and around, neatly tying him to the pole like a string shish kebab.

While the crane's friends unwrapped him, I gave Natalie the scoop on Waldo.

She frowned and cocked her head. "So if it's not him, then who's the zombie master?"

"I can't say his name, but his initials are: Cool Beans."

"The librarian?"

"The same." I led Natalie away from the line. "He knows too much about zombies. It's time we found out what's behind that closed door in the library."

We strode across the grass. Near the library steps, Natalie and I slowed to let a small herd of kids cross our path.

Tony Newt, Bo's twin brother, leaned from the crowd. "Hey, Chet!" he said. "Check this out. It's the latest thing."

He waved some boxy toy at me. But I had no time for fun and frolic. Danger was blooming like zits on a junk-food junkie.

Tony and his group tromped down the hall. At the library door, Natalie grabbed my shoulder.

"Wait," she said. "Just how are we gonna get in there? And when we do, how are we gonna stop him? That's one jumbo-sized possum, Chet."

"Hah!" I said. "Would Sam Spade let some big lug scare him? Would Sherlock Holmes worry about having a plan?"

Natalie nodded. "Yes," she said, "they would."

I paused. "Okay . . . then, let's——"

Rrrinnng! went the class bell.

"——investigate it at lunch," I said.

Natalie sniggered. "Good plan."

10

Roofless Behavior

The only problem with lunch is that you have to suffer through history class to get to it. Don't take me wrong, it's usually one of my better subjects. (History, I mean, not lunch. Lunch isn't a subject; it's a higher calling.)

But Mr. Ratnose's history class could make an ancient Roman start roamin' again.

I put the time to good use, pondering how Natalie and I were going to get into the library's locked room. We could try the simple approach, of course: Knock on the door, then improvise.

Simple, but also a good way to get captured.

Or we could create a diversion. Set off a stink bomb in the library and sneak in while everyone was—

"*Psst,* Chet!"

"Huh?" I looked up to see Sammy the weasel toss me a folded note. I caught it with my tongue. The paper tasted of crayons and chalk.

Psst, Chett! Isn't this Dullsville? How wud you like to com over to my house todday for snacks? It'll be funn!!!
   —Sammy

I was no spelling whiz, but even I could see that Sammy's spelling wasn't exactly minding its p's and q's. But never mind.

I gave him the thumbs-up. Sammy grinned. I figured I could wrap up the case at lunch and still have plenty of time to goof off after school.

Boy, was I dreaming.

After a third helping of centipede burritos (hey, it pays to befriend the cafeteria ladies), I was ready to rock and roll. Or at least dance the Hokey Pokey.

I snagged Natalie and explained my plan, on the way to the library.

"Okay," she said doubtfully, "if you're sure."

"Natalie, when have I ever steered you wrong?"

She shot me a look. "You want the full list, or just the Reader's Digest highlights?"

"Ha, ha," I said. We stood beside the library. "Now, easy does it."

Natalie flapped lazily to the roof of the building. I scuttled up the wall, no sweat. In my line of work, it pays to be a lizard.

We began searching the rooftop for a heating vent or skylight.

"If we can catch him in the act," I said, "we'll have the proof we need to put Cool Beans out of business."

Natalie sniffed and fanned a wing. "Speaking of beans, Chet, I wish you hadn't gone for that third burrito."

Just then, I spotted a likely-looking hump on the roof. "Hello, what's this?"

Natalie joined me near the skylight. "Bingo!" she said.

We crept toward the edge of the glass panel. Moving slower than the last lap of an arctic-slug race, I eased forward until I could check out the room below. I blinked in surprise.

"Yuck!" I said. "Don't they ever clean these windows?"

The skylight was crudded over with a thick coating of scuzz and grime. It was about as see-through as a pair of lead underpants.

Natalie brushed a wing across the surface. No effect. I rubbed with my coat sleeve. The grease smeared, but we still couldn't see into the locked room.

"Well, at least they can't see us, either," said Natalie. "Let's try listening in."

She leaned onto the skylight and pressed her cheek to the smudged glass.

"Hear anything?" I asked. "What are they saying?"

"They say, *'Roblgiv snorggle zzshvbble zhnovv.'*" She imitated the sound of muffled voices. Mockingbirds can be a real hoot sometimes.

"Here, let me try," I said, nudging her aside and crawling onto the skylight.

"Chet, I don't think you—"

"Relax, willya?" I snaked toward the middle and put my ear to the glass. "This skylight is strong enough to handle heavy weather; it's strong enough to handle us."

The sound was clearer toward the middle. I heard, *So what do you think he meant by . . .* craaackkk.

"*'Craaackkk'?*" I muttered. "What's—"

C-r-a-a-a-c-k-k-k! went the skylight.

Oh.

The glass buckled like a bawling bully in Principal Zero's office. As I plummeted downward, the last thing I saw was Natalie's worried face.

Bomf!

In a spray of glass and grime, I hit the tabletop. *Ooooch.* The extra burritos rearranged themselves in my aching gut.

As landings go, it was a doozy. But I thought the East German judges might take off a few points for my style.

I shook my head to clear it. My breath came back in a wheeze, and I checked out the room.

The big round table was littered with books and glass chunks. Half the kids had jumped to their feet. The rest sat and stared like puppets with their strings cut. Zombies!

Too late for them, but maybe I could save the others.

"Run for your lives!" I shouted. "He's trying to turn you into zombies!"

A big fifth-grade owl blinked at me. "Who?" he asked.

You get that from owls.

I staggered to my feet, shaking glass from my coat and hat. "Cool Beans, that's who. He's hypnotizing you for evil purposes."

"Evil porpoises?" A deep voice chuckled behind me. "Why, I don't even have any grumpy dolphins. You're wiggin' out, Winston."

Cool Beans stepped through the open door.

"Nice try, mister," I said. I waved an arm at the stupefied students. "We know all about your little zombie factory."

The librarian chortled again and put his massive paws on his hips.

I clenched my fists and readied for action.

"Don't blow a gasket, daddy-o," said Cool Beans. He surveyed the room with sleepy eyes. "You just, heh, *dropped in* on my extra-credit book club."

Book club?

"And now," purred a different voice, "won't you drop in on my office?" I knew that voice, and I didn't like it.

Behind the librarian, a broad belly poked through the doorway. A fat cat head followed. It was Principal Zero, wearing his someone's-gonna-get-it expression.

I could guess who that someone was.

His whiskers bristled as he thrust a broom and dustpan at me, then pointed at the glass fragments. "Shall we say, in ten minutes?"

Shall we say, on the twelfth of never? I thought. But you don't tell that to an angry principal.

You just grin, sweep, and bear it.

11

A Big Stink from the Head Cheese

There are two theories on how to argue with a principal. Neither one works.

"But that book club is just a front for his zombie operation," I said.

Principal Zero's claws kneaded his scarred desktop. "Nonsense," he rumbled. "Aloyicious Theonlyest Bunk is the most respected librarian in town. Neither he nor anyone else at this school is, as you put it, turning students into zombies."

"But—"

"Gecko, the only reason I'm not giving you a month of detention—and believe me, I want to—is that Mr. Bunk has asked me to pardon you." Principal Zero sniffed. "He's more lenient with the students than I am."

I tried another approach. "Look, Mr. Zero. Every day, I see more and more zombies around school. *Somebody's* making them."

He smoothed the fur on his jowls and watched me with narrowed eyes, the way I watch a horsefly I'm planning to lunch on. "I see," he said. "And how do you know they're zombies?"

"They walk like zombies, they talk like zombies..." I gripped the edge of the desktop. "They speak only when spoken to, and they even clean the blackboards."

Principal Zero smiled a Cheshire cat smile. Or the smile that the Cheshire cat would've worn if he'd been an overweight pussycat with a bad attitude.

"You, Chet Gecko, are a deluded troublemaker. You see good students, and you think they're zombies." Mr. Zero's tail twitched. He snarled, "If you know what's good for you, you'll drop this case."

My mouth fell open. "Drop it?" I said. "But my—"

"Drop it now," said Principal Zero. "Or I'll drop you so fast you'll bounce."

His tail twitched faster, back and forth, like a cockeyed cobra getting ready to strike.

"Is that all?" I asked.

His fangs gleamed. "Let me give you a friendly

piece of advice, Chet Gecko. Now would be a good time to keep your nose clean."

"Anything else?"

"Yes. Don't talk with your mouth full...keep your elbows off the table...never eat a dish called Chef's Surprise..."

He was worse than my mother. I slowly backed from the room as Principal Zero rambled on.

Lunch was over; kids were back in class. I dawdled through the halls while that bowl of soggy Froot Loops I call my brain puzzled over this confusing case.

So Waldo wasn't the zombie master. And according to Principal Zero—if I believed him—neither was Cool Beans.

Then who was? And how was he, she, or it turning my classmates into zombies?

And on top of all that, *why* were they doing it?

My head hurt. This was harder than my bogus science project of turning chocolate to gold. (I needn't have bothered; chocolate is more valuable, anyway.)

Where was Natalie when I needed her brainpower? In class, that's where. She'd flown the coop when I got in trouble. Some partner.

With these thoughts tumbling through my mind

like a woodchuck in a washing machine, of course I bumped into the second-to-last person I wanted to see.

Meena Moe.

She clutched a hall pass in one delicate paw. Her expression was anything but delicate.

"Chet Gecko!" she said.

"Where?" I asked.

Meena *harrumph*ed. (At least I think she harrumphed. It sounded more like a gopher snake choking on a gum ball.) "None of your foolishness," she said. "Why have you not reported to me?"

"Not much to report," I said. "Yes, your sister's a zombie. And no, I don't know how she got that way or how to cure her."

Meena's eyes grew big. She gasped, "I knew it! Poor Eena." She twisted the hall pass in her paws. "You must help her. Can you discover how to restore her to normalcy?"

Normalcy? Is that how fifth graders talk? If so, I wasn't looking forward to my next year of school.

I scratched my chin. "I don't know. That's a pretty tough nut to crack."

"I don't care a fig for nuts," she said. "If you can cure Eena, I'll give you a special bonus."

This sounded interesting. "Like what?" I asked.

Meena eyed my belly and made a small, very

small, smile. "How about all the mosquito milk shakes you can drink?"

For a goody-goody, this guinea pig was a shrewd bargainer.

"Done," I said. I eyed her book bag. "Now, how's about a down payment?"

12

To Dream the Im-possum-ble Dream

The rest of the school day slipped by in a haze of geology and gum (Meena had parted with fifty cents for a snack). Still steamed at my partner, I spent recess avoiding Natalie.

But I did revisit the library. Despite Mr. Zero's guarantees, something was funny about Cool Beans.

I turned the knob. The library door swung silently open.

And there he was.

The huge possum was slumped at his desk in the dimness, lively as a statue of cool carved from an iceberg. I strolled closer, keeping a wary eye out.

Was he napping? Or zombified?

"Uh, Cool Beans?" I said.

No response.

Was he breathing? I couldn't tell.

I scanned the mess on his desktop for clues. A handful of jazz CDs...a bag of gourmet coffee...a pile of papers and letters...a glossy eight-by-ten photo autographed by someone named Kilometers Davis...and near the librarian's right hand, a thick book: *Understanding the Undead.*

Hmm. Where had this treasure come from? I reached for it.

Fwump! A furry paw shot out, pinning my hand to the desk.

"Well, hidey-ho," said Cool Beans.

Yikes! My tail almost fell off in surprise. I should've known. He'd been playing possum.

I struggled but had about as much effect as an inchworm arm wrestling a two-ton gorilla.

"Let...me...go!" I cried.

One fuzzy finger found its way to his lips. *"Shh,"* said Cool Beans. "It's a library, daddy-o."

I stopped fighting.

"That's better." He squinted at me. "Now, lemme guess. You're trackin' down a zombie master, and you think I'm it."

I nodded.

"Man, are you playin' on the wrong set of bongos," he said.

"Oh, yeah? Then how come you know so much about zombies and the undead?"

Cool Beans grinned a syrup-slow grin. "My roots, man. Down South, where I come from, the bayou's lousy with zombies, werewolves, encyclopedia salesmen, and other freaks of nature."

I frowned. "And what about your so-called book club? Half the students were zombies."

"Yeah, I dug that action," he said, "and I wondered, *Hey, what gives?*" Cool Beans shook his head. "Tell you somethin' else: I never had such a good turnout before, either. Crazy, man."

He gave me a level look, then released my hand. I nodded thanks.

"Cool your heels, comrade, and check this out,"

said the big possum. He snagged a chair with his tail and slid it toward me.

I cooled my heels.

Cool Beans opened the book. "You were lookin' to find out what, exactly?"

"How do you unmake a zombie?" I said.

He flipped through the book. "Well, as I recall, to *make* a zombie, you hafta either hypnotize 'em or steal their soul," he said. "So to *un*make 'em . . . aha!"

Cool Beans stabbed a thick finger onto the page.

"What?" I asked.

He pinched his fingers together. "A flea. Man, I hate those buggers." Cool Beans brought the flea to his mouth and turned it into a quick snack. "Now, where was I?"

I prompted him. "A zombie cure?"

The librarian turned some more pages. "Alrighty-ro," he said. "Here we go. To unmake zombies who've been raised from the dead, you gotta ace their master."

"Ace him?" I asked.

Cool Beans drew a finger across his throat in the traditional croak-'em gesture.

"Oh," I said. "Um, what about a zombie who until recently was a living, breathing third grader?"

He turned the page. "Let's see . . . to cure a live one, you gotta either make a counterhypnosis spell or break the talisman."

"Talisman? What's that, a Lithuanian breakfast bar?"

"Naw, you know," said Cool Beans, "a charm, a juju, an amulet. Some powerful thing that holds the magic. When you break it, the zombie goes back to normal."

"Riiight," I said. Somehow, I could believe in zombies, but when you start talking magical doo-dads, I get skeptical. Go figure.

I stood up. "Listen, it's been a slice of heaven, but I gotta go find a zombie master. Thanks for the low-down. And, uh, sorry about the skylight."

The librarian grinned. "It's four bars past cool, *kemosabe*. Catch you on the flip side, man."

I pushed open the library door and blinked at the sunshine. As my eyes adjusted, I scouted the scene. Things were worse than I'd thought.

Most students motored along like goody-goodies on wheels. One carried a teacher's books. Another helped a janitor paint over graffiti. A bunch of them sat in a circle, studying together.

It was quiet. Too quiet.

Where were the hair-pullings, the dirt-clod fights, the breathless chases of dear old Emerson Hicky?

What the heck was happening to my school?

13

The Squeaky Weasel Gets the Grease

"What's happenin', Chet?" It was Sammy the weasel, standing in the shade with a shorter, prettier weasel. She looked enough like him to be his little sister.

"Meet my little sister, Sandy," said Sammy.

Those detective instincts—uncanny, yes?

I joined them. It seemed that little third grader Sandy was having a birthday party that afternoon. So *that's* why Sammy was trying to get me to his house.

With my usual grace, I tried to slip out of it.

"Look, I know I said I'd come over, but the case I'm on is pretty tough. It's taking longer than I thought."

Sammy frowned. Sandy pulled a long face and said, "But we're having ice cream and caaake..."

Cake? "What kind?"

"Jamocha almond earwig with strawberry frosting," said Sammy, twirling his tail idly. "Too bad you'll miss it."

I rubbed my stomach. It growled pitifully. "Well, maybe I can drop by for just a little bite—er, bit," I said.

Sandy clapped her hands and beamed. Her brother said, "That's cooler than Eskimo eyebrows."

"Yeah, whatever." His metaphors were starting to bug me.

On a scrap of paper, Sammy sketched a quick map to his house. "Right after school," he said. "Don't forget."

My stomach grumbled again. I wouldn't forget.

As I strolled off pondering the case, the bell rang. Time to face my last classes of the day. But whatever they held, it couldn't be tougher than the mystery I was gnawing on.

As I half listened to Mr. Ratnose's blather, I turned over the facts in my mind.

Fact: The zombie population was booming. Fact: If the zombie master wasn't using hypnosis, then he or she had some magic gizmo that could steal souls.

Fact: If I didn't manage to do at least some of my

homework, I might have to spend another year in fourth grade with Mr. Ratnose.

I started paying attention.

At long last, the final bell rang. The game was afoot!

Unfortunately, the zombie master knew all the rules; I barely knew which game we were playing. Following the flow of my classmates, I left my seat and scuffed out the door.

Someone tugged at my sleeve.

"Ur, Chet?" said Waldo the furball. "Can we talk?"

"Okay, but make it snappy," I said. "I'm a busy gecko."

We braved the tide of homeward-bound students and stepped out onto the grass. Waldo glanced quickly from side to side. He probably wanted to invite me to his next magic show.

"Chet, remember how you told me to watch for anything shady?" he muttered, barely moving his lips.

Oh great, a furball detective.

"Yeah," I said. "So?"

Waldo grabbed my arm. "I saw something. It was Fred-o the muskrat. He's been lurking around a lot lately."

I chuckled. "Probably just wants your lunch money."

"No, I'm serious," he said. Waldo frowned. "I watch Fred-o going around with this bag, see? I can't tell whether he's taking something or giving it. But he's seen lots of students today."

I paused. Maybe it was nothing. But maybe Fred-o was wrapped up in this zombie thing somehow.

"Thanks," I said. "You're a good furball, Waldo."

He beamed. I started off.

"Hey, Chet," he said. "Where ya headed? Tracking down clues?"

"Naw, just some shindig at Sammy's house. Then, it's back to work."

Waldo gave me the big eyes. "Can I come along?" he asked. "I could entertain with my magic act. Or I could pick up clues at Sammy's."

I hid a smile with my hand. "Sorry, kiddo. The only clues you'd find would be cake crumbs on my coat."

Waldo's face fell. I clapped his shoulder. "Just keep your eyes peeled, and I'll see you around."

I headed for the bushes at the edge of campus where I always stash my skateboard. As I bent to retrieve it, a voice growled behind me.

"Gecko, get your tail in my office," it said.

Principal Zero!

I whirled to find Natalie grinning at me.

"Very funny," I said. "That mockingbird trick is gonna get you in deep dingleberries someday."

She shrugged and groomed a wing feather. "Anything for a giggle."

I frowned. "I guess so. Did you have a good laugh when I landed in hot water at the library?"

"Actually, you landed on your—"

My glare silenced her.

Natalie shifted from foot to foot. She didn't meet my eye. "Uh, sorry about that, Chet," she said at last. "I figured it wouldn't help any if both of us were busted by the principal."

"You did, huh?"

"Look, let's forget about it," she said. "Come on, time to hunt up that zombie master."

I sniffed. "Can't right now. I'm busy." I set the skateboard down. "Maybe later."

"What?" Natalie cocked her head. "Too busy to investigate? That's not like you. What's going on?"

I hopped on my board and pushed off down the sidewalk. "Can't talk; gotta go," I said.

Before turning the corner I glanced back. Natalie was still standing there, wearing a puzzled look. Waldo was hustling up to her.

Fine. They could have each other—I didn't need any fair-weather assistant detectives.

I knew what I needed, so I hustled off to Sammy's house. As the saying goes, a friend with cake is a good friend to make.

Or something like that.

14

Sibling Revelry

After ten minutes of zigging and zagging through streets packed with carpooling kids and frazzled parents, I ended up in Sammy's neighborhood. The street boasted huge mansions squeezed in beside each other like a bakery case full of double-decker angel food cakes.

This was Sammy's block?

I checked the address again: 1923 Hifalutin Lane. It was the kind of neighborhood that put the *hoity* in *hoity-toity*.

My skateboard carried me up to the wrought-iron gates. They were open, so I parked my chariot under a nearby hedge and strolled up the driveway.

The front yard was okay, if you like an immaculate lawn the size of two football fields. And the house was all right, too. It wasn't quite as big as the Taj Mahal, and it didn't have as many windows as the Empire State Building, but a modest family could live there in a pinch.

Long-stemmed flowers the color of Easter candy lined the walkway like Broadway chorus girls about to burst into a verse of "Oh! Susanna." I reached for the doorbell.

But before I could ring, the door eased open to reveal Sammy.

"Hey," he said.

"Hey, yourself," I replied. This gecko is always fast with a comeback.

"Glad you made it. Come on in."

I stepped into an entry hall large enough to hold a couple of good-sized blimps with room left over for the *Queen Mary*.

"You sure this place is big enough?" I asked. "What if the Mongrel Horde shows up for dinner?"

Sammy chuckled. "Yeah, it's a bit much. But we're a big family."

He led me across acres of plush carpet. It was deep enough to swallow a small herd of elephants. We passed rooms where I glimpsed marble statues of old Greek guys, pretty paintings by dead French guys, and enough fancy knickknacks to choke a medium-sized horse.

"If I get lost," I said, "should I fire off a flare or wait for the search party?"

Sammy tossed a smile over his shoulder. "Almost there," he warbled.

Finally, we approached a room that rang with the happy babble of kids partying.

"She'll love that you showed up," said Sammy. "My sister's got a big crush on you."

I wrinkled my nose. "*Eeew.* Now you tell me. Cake-and-cooties is a dish I can do without."

"Relax, willya?"

I eyeballed the room. Just slightly bigger than your average airplane hangar, it held scads of fancy furniture and sculpture, and a fireplace big enough to roast a hockey team or two. A cuckoo clock on the mantelpiece featured a monkey and a weasel chasing each other around a track.

A classy touch, I thought.

About thirty kids, from kindergartners through sixth graders, laughed and frolicked throughout the room, playing birthday-type games.

In the thick of the crowd, I spotted Meena Moe, my guinea pig client. She wore a frown that said, *Why are you here partying when you should be figuring out how to dezombify my sister?*

I offered a guilty smile and wondered the same thing myself. Then the party scene reclaimed my attention.

Things were heating up as the sugary treats took effect. Nine or ten weasels wove in and out of the action, carrying cups of punch, passing out candy, and generally playing host. Sammy's family, I guessed.

"Oh, hiii, Chet!" said Sandy, the birthday girl. She gave a little finger wave and blew me a kiss.

I ducked.

"You just missed our pin-the-tail-on-the-cat game," said Sammy.

On one ice-blue wall, I saw a drawing of Principal Zero's broad behind, with a crooked tail pinned to one side. Pinholes pockmarked that ample derriere.

You had to admire their sense of humor.

"Look, it's Rita," said Sammy. "Cake time!"

A tall weasel in a maid's apron burst through another door, wheeling a tray that wobbled under a truly mammoth earwig cake dripping with frosting.

Yum. Was this the cake that launched a thousand lips? Mine started twitching. I couldn't wait to wrap my mouth around a piece (or four).

We circled Sandy and sang "Happy Birthday." To my untrained ear, we sounded just like the Vienna Boys Choir being fed into a sausage machine.

As the birthday weasel blew out the candles, I happened to glance across the circle. What I saw punctured my enthusiasm like a pin in a whoopee cushion.

There, at the back of the pack, lurked Fred-o the

muskrat, a sneaky snaggletoothed smile on his ugly mug.

What was that punk doing here?

Fred-o was a wasp in the ice cream of life, a stink bomb in the toilet of happiness. Trouble stuck to him like dumb on a dingbat.

And I knew that the party was about to get a lot more lively.

15

It's My Party and I'll Pry If I Want To

After collecting a hefty piece of earwig cake, I sat beside Sammy on the couch. I glared at Fred-o the muskrat.

"*Mmf*... why's that... *mmfw*... wrong-o at your party?" I asked around a massive mouthful.

Sammy glanced where I was looking. "You mean Fred-o? He's no wrong-o; he's just misunderstood."

"Yeah. He's misunderstood, like I'm the queen of the quahogs."

"Look, your majesty, I hate to burst your bubble," said Sammy, "but he's actually a nice guy underneath."

It was fruitless to argue with the weasel. Friendship had blinded him.

"Okay," I said. "If you say so."

I checked out all the happy kids feeding their faces. No zombies in sight, so I relaxed a little.

Still, I kept a wary eye on Fred-o while polishing off my cake and licking the plate. When he made his move, I'd be waiting.

Before I could grab a second piece, the maid reappeared. This time, she staggered under a box big enough to hide a Shetland pony and his sister. Fred-o helped her carry it.

"Party favors, everyone!" grunted lovely Rita, weasel maid.

The guests flocked to the box like raging moms at a bargain basement sale, elbowing one another and grabbing. Sammy's siblings helped pass out the presents, which turned out to be handheld video games—the latest Weasel Boy, I had no doubt.

Sammy handed me a game. "Here, Chet. This is for you, from Sandy."

I eyed the gizmo. "I thought the birthday girl was supposed to get the gifts."

"Not in this family," he said. "Dad says that giving is better than receiving. Enjoy!"

With that bit of Santa Clausian philosophy, he moved on to pass out more party favors. *Oohs*, *aahs*, and *cools* followed in Sammy's wake.

All over the room, kids plopped down with their new toys.

Beep-bop boop, came from one corner.

Beep-bop boop, answered from another corner.

Soon the room reverberated with more *beep-bops* than a robot class reunion. Nearly everyone was playing a video game, cake and candies forgotten.

I inspected the crowd for Fred-o the muskrat. He'd disappeared.

I looked at my empty plate, then at the game. Three guesses which interested me more (and the first two don't count). I started to rise.

A paw touched my shoulder.

"Don't you like my present?" Sandy stood behind the couch, pouting like an Olympic finalist in the sulk marathon.

"Uh, sure, I . . ."

"I picked it out just for you," she wheedled. "Won't you try it?" She took my plate, saying, "I'll get you seconds."

I shrugged and turned on the game. It couldn't hurt to play a quick round before I finished my cake and went to find Fred-o.

The tiny screen lit up, spelling out MYSTERY BUSTERS in green letters.

Hmm, not too boring. Using the buttons, I guided a detective character into a haunted house and walked him down the halls.

Over the game's beeping came the chatter of more kids showing up at the door. The party was growing. But somehow, I couldn't tear my eyes off the screen.

The little detective on my game screen tramped back and forth... back and forth... down, down, down...

This wasn't like any video game I'd ever played.

Sights, sounds, and sensations faded away. The whole world narrowed to the tiny screen.

My eyelids started sinking like the *Titanic*'s last lifeboat—the one with the hole in it. I was sliding into a dark, deep, haunted place from which no detective ever returns.

I didn't know it, but I was about three heartbeats away from falling into The Big Nap.

And I couldn't lift a finger to stop myself.

16

Zombie Jamboree

*F*a-*tchoom!*

Something furry hit the video game and sent it flying from my hands.

I blinked. Each eyelid felt as thick and heavy as a triple-decker whale blubber sandwich. Echoing through a tunnel came a strangely familiar voice.

"Hurry, hurry, hurry! Step right up! The magic is about to begin."

I blinked again. This time, my eyelids moved easier. My brain still felt like lukewarm oatmeal. It sent an order to my eyes.

Like rusty wheels, my eyeballs obeyed. They turned left and saw a big furry butt.

I knew that butt.

It spoke again, clearer this time. "Ladies and jelly-spoons, boys and grills, prepare yourself for feats of presto-digitation like you've never seen before. *Hur, hur.*"

A talking butt?

My head wobbled on its neck like a broken-down jack-in-the-box on a spring. Before me rose a furry back, a furry head, and above that, a ratty-looking top hat.

"I am the Great Waldini," said Waldo. "And for my first trick, I'll need three common objects."

He grabbed a couple of video games from the limp paws of two mice. They blinked vacantly. Waldo plucked a banana from a nearby fruit bowl.

His juggling was pretty pathetic. Twice, Waldo missed the banana and knocked some kid's cake flying.

"Hey! We didn't order a magician." It was Fred-o the muskrat, back in the game. His eyes narrowed suspiciously.

Feeling was flowing back into my body like a milk shake into a glass. I shifted and scanned the room. Most of the kids were still staring, hypnotized, at their video games. A handful watched Waldo.

Fred-o and the weasels had gathered into a knot at the back of the room. They frowned like a pack of vice principals uncovering vice.

Time to move.

I lurched to my feet. "Ladies and germs, for his next trick, the Great Waldini will do his famous disappearing act."

Waldo shot me a puzzled frown. "Ur, what do you mean?" he whispered. "I'm just getting started."

I grabbed Waldo by the elbow. "Everyone, please close your eyes and count to three," I said. "One...two..." Those who weren't hypnotized still stared at us.

So much for that trick.

I looked out the window and gasped like a soap-opera star just before a commercial. "Look, it's... it's...the Mighty Maguffin!"

That did it. As everybody turned to look, I stumbled rubber-legged into the hall, with Waldo in tow. We waded through the thick carpeting toward (I hoped) the door. I wished I'd left a trail of bread crumbs.

"W-what's the big idea?" said Waldo. "I was a hit. I was killing that audience."

"Yeah. And if you'd stayed, they would've killed *you*."

Waldo pouted. I staggered. We came to a fork in the hallway—right or left?

"Which way's it gonna be, buster?" someone said. I stepped forward.

"Natalie!" I cried.

She leaned against the wall of the right-hand corridor with an easy smirk. "Well, it ain't Trey Bien, the French Fried Potato Bug," said Natalie.

Angry voices clamored behind us.

"Sounds like I'm just in time to save your bacon," she said. "Good thing I followed you. I had a feeling..."

"Hold that feeling," I said. "And let's go!"

She pointed along the right passageway, and we trotted down its winding length.

"Does all this have something to do with Zombie Central?" asked Natalie. She flapped just above us—the hallway was that wide.

"Yup," I said. "Waldo was right. Fred-o is the zombie master, and he's tricked these poor weasels into helping him."

Waldo gaped. "I was right?"

"They're using video games to turn kids into zombies—stealing their souls somehow."

"Me?" said Waldo. He grinned hugely. "I was right?"

"This ain't no time for ticker tape parades, furball. We gotta find the door, pronto!"

We skidded around a corner—*whumpf!*—right into a tall weasel wearing a white lab coat. Round glasses covered his eyes, and a fancy stethoscope

dangled from his neck. Even though we'd bumped him, the weasel stayed as calm and unruffled as a cement pond.

Sammy's dad! He'd soon put a stop to this spooky business.

"Uh, Mr. Weasel," I said.

"That's *Viesél*," he replied in a voice smooth as fresh chocolate milk.

"You don't know me, but I'm Sammy's friend."

He nodded and smiled. "Mmm, indeed?"

Voices echoed down the hall, drawing closer.

"Listen, this evil muskrat zombie master has corrupted your kids. He's using them to turn my classmates into zombies. You gotta stop it."

Mr. Viesél's bristly eyebrows inched up slightly. "He's corrupting my children? Well, well." For a concerned father, he didn't look too concerned.

"Chet's telling the truth," said Natalie.

The tall weasel nodded again. His bushy tail twitched. "Oh, I believe him," he said, "except for one small detail."

I frowned. "What's that?" I asked.

"You see, my children are corrupting Fred-o." Mr. Viesél's glasses twinkled. "And actually, *I'm* the zombie master."

Darn.

17

What's the Hubbub, Bub?

He reached for us, grinning like Dracula's dentist on National Cavity Day. Behind us, shouts rang in the hall, "There they are!"

Once again, my gecko reflexes saved me. Almost before I could think, I found myself halfway up tne wall, scrambling out of reach.

The tall weasel tried to follow, but he slid back down the smooth surface and landed with a thump. "Oh, bother!" he said.

Natalie flapped airborne. In the confusion, Waldo slipped past Mr. Viesél and trucked on down the hall, top hat and all.

Our pursuers appeared: The big muskrat and several weasels.

Mr. Viesél barked orders. "Fred-o, Shi-Shi, and Sylvester," he said, "go get that ... that—whatever it is." He pointed in the direction Waldo had taken. The muskrat and two weasels trotted off.

I climbed farther up the wall. Natalie perched on a nearby chandelier.

"Sheena and Santiago," said Mr. Viesél, "go fetch the zombies. Sammy, you stay with me."

Natalie raised an eyebrow. "Shi-Shi, Sylvester, Sheena, and Santiago?" she muttered. "What kind of cruel dad are you?"

"I heard that," said Mr. Viesél. He and Sammy glared up at us. Their eyes were colder than the Ice Queen's tootsies. "Don't mock my family," he growled. "Family is everything."

"So," said Sammy. "The great detective and his partner, caught like cockroaches in a roach motel."

"Hah!" I said. "You haven't got your hands on us yet." I sneered at him. I can give good sneer when the occasion demands. "You're quite the little actor, Sammy boy. I almost fell for it."

Mr. Viesél rubbed his paws together. "Enough chatter. Soon I will steal your immortal souls, so you might as well surrender and make it easy on yourselves."

I crawled farther along the wall, away from Natalie. The weasels followed.

"If we're making things easy," I said, "then why not tell me why you're turning Emerson Hicky into Zombieville?"

The tall weasel chuckled. "Why not, indeed?" he said. "We're actually doing the parents and teachers a service."

I snorted. "A service? Sure, every mom wants her kid to grow up to be a zombie. It's the good ol' American way."

"Every mother wants her child to listen up and do well in school," said Mr. Viesél. "And zombies are very obedient..."

"Yeah," I said. "They obey *you*." I edged farther down the hall; weasel father and son stayed with me.

"We just order them to study hard, help their teachers, and be nice to their parents," Sammy said.

Our little group had wandered away from Natalie. She shot me a question with her eyes. I gave a small nod.

"So," I said to Mr. Viesél, "you're doing some kind of community service, eh? That stinks like leftover junebug casserole. What's your angle?"

Mr. Viesél smoothed the fur on his sleek belly. "Well, there's no flies on you."

I blinked. "Of course not. I eat 'em."

"I mean you catch on quickly," said Mr. Viesél.

"Yes, this community service, as you put it, does turn a tidy profit for us. You see, well-behaved children earn healthy allowances..."

I sidled a little farther down the hall. Then I heard it: A strange shambling sound, coming from beyond Natalie. "And well-behaved zombies give their allowance money to you," I said.

"Precisely. And now, I must ask you to—"

"One last question," I said, "for old times' sake. Where's the magic talisman that powers the video games?"

The shuffling drew closer. It sounded just around the corner.

Mr. Viesél glanced at Sammy. They laughed. "Surely," said the tall weasel, "you don't expect me to spill all my secrets, like some third-rate villain in a Hollywood action movie?"

"You were doing pretty good so far," I said. "Why stop now?"

I glanced back toward Natalie and saw the source of the noise. A small zombie army had just rounded the corner, stepping stiff-legged, with hollow, haunted stares.

"Go, Natalie!" I shouted. "Get some help! I'll keep these mugs busy."

She launched herself from the chandelier with one last worried look behind. Natalie flapped over the heads of the zombie crew, heading for an open window somewhere.

I turned my attention to the gang below. It looked like about forty to one. Not good odds, even for a muscle-bound action hero. And I was no action hero.

The gathering crowd included a stupefied Meena Moe. Great. If I didn't cure her zombiehood, I wouldn't even get paid for this creepy caper.

But then, why worry about pay, with a hall full of hostile ghouls before me? I eyeballed the group.

I was safe, as long as there weren't any wall-climbing lizard or frog zombies on hand.

Mr. Viesél surveyed his gang. "You, you, and you," he pointed at two chameleons and a tree frog, "go fetch me that gecko."

Uh-oh.

Time for this gecko to exit, stage left.

18

Amulet, Prince of Denmark

The frog and lizards climbed the wall in zombie time—slow but steady. I scuttled before them as fast as I could scut.

The zombie trio cut off any retreat. The weasels and the rest of their soulless gang paced below on foot.

I glanced ahead. The wall was ending. What waited beyond it?

I whipped around the corner, nearly losing my grip. But luck was with me. The hall opened up into a three-story stairwell.

While Mr. Viesél and company panted up the stairs, I zipped up the wall to the third level. Now I had a head start.

Leaping to the landing, I dashed along the third story, desperately seeking magic amulets, secret hiding places, or the odd cavalry troop to rescue me. If I could just destroy that magic gizmo, the odds would even up a bit.

If. That was a pretty big *if.*

Shouts echoed behind me as the weasels ordered their mob to spread out. What do you call a group of the undead, anyway? A gaggle of ghouls? A snarl of zombies?

I popped in and out of rooms like a prairie dog on a pogo stick. Anything remotely talismanical got the heave-ho.

A statue of a sad-eyed clown? *Kittssch!* It smashed against the wall.

An enamel Easter egg? *Skronnch!* It shattered on a baseboard.

A carved hand mirror? *Skrassh!* Better seven years of bad luck than a lifetime as a zombie.

Unfortunately, I couldn't tell if I'd broken the right gewgaw until I took a gander at the zombie search party—and if they saw me first, I'd be weasel bait.

At the next set of stairs, I took my one-gecko hurricane down to the second floor. I had just hoisted the bust of some old Greek guy, when a slight sound made me turn.

Mr. Viesél!

"Do you know why the fisherwoman married the flounder?" I asked.

"Eh?" he said.

"Because he was such a great *catch*!" I shouted, tossing the sculpture at him.

I shot from the room, with the weasel in hot pursuit. Down the stairs we scrambled.

"Zombies, to me!" he bellowed.

I raced along the hallway. My breath came in gasps. Starting tomorrow, I promised myself, I'd lay off the candy-coated wasps.

Assuming I made it to tomorrow.

I rounded a corner and found myself back in the room where the party had started. Two zombie toads stood beside the other door. They spotted me and shambled forward. Mr. Viesél was only a few steps behind.

I desperately scanned the room, and my eyes fixed on the monkey-and-weasel clock above the fireplace. *The talisman?*

Quick as a monkey after a you-know-what, I flashed to the mantelpiece and lifted the clock high.

"Noooo!" cried Mr. Viesél, with his arms outstretched.

Ka-shazzz!

The timepiece shattered on the hearth.

"That...was a family heirloom," snarled Mr. Viesél. "But not the talisman."

Sammy dashed into the doorway and cut off my escape route.

"Hold him!" he told the zombies. Before I could leap for the wall, they grabbed my arms.

My goose was cooked.

At their master's command, the zombies carried me over to a nearby table and pinned me down. Mr. Viesél picked up a video game and held it before me.

"Now, watch closely," he murmured in that chocolatey voice. The tall weasel pressed the buttons and SUPER MEATBALL BROS. appeared in green letters on the small screen. Sammy held my head so I couldn't look away.

But as I struggled against his grip, my attention was drawn by something dangling behind the game—Mr. Viesél's stethoscope.

Mystical figures and strange runes crawled all over it. If this was a stethoscope, I was Dr. Feelgood.

The magic soul-stealing talisman!

Quick as a roadrunner's rest stop, I shot out my tongue and—*sluuurrp!*—pulled the amulet into my mouth. Its chain broke like a store-bought gingersnap.

"Hey!" shouted Mr. Viesél.

At that moment, an amplified voice rang forth

from outside. "Attention, this is the police! We have the house surrounded. Come out with your hands up!"

Sammy's paws loosened as he glanced up at the window, distracted. I seized my chance. Like a hall-of-fame loogey hawker, I twisted my head and spat the talisman toward the fireplace.

It sailed, end over end, in a sweet arc.

Mr. Viesél watched, horrified.

Bimp. The talisman landed gently in a rat zombie's outstretched paw.

Drat that rat.

Mr. Viesél grinned. "Now, where were we?"

"*Hur, hur, hur,* thought you could ditch me, eh?" Waldo slouched into the room and right up beside the rat zombie.

"Waldo, you don't—" I began.

"No more foolin'," he said. "This time I'm doing a real trick, and everybody's gonna watch. Now, I'll need some sort of household object..." Waldo plucked the amulet from the rat's paw. "Thank you."

The weasels and zombies stared dumfounded as my furball classmate wrapped the magic talisman in a grimy handkerchief, put it on a chair, and waved his hand over it

"Alla-kazmallah and shibbidy-shmear, make this

doodad disappear!" he shouted. Waldo gave a half bow to the left and to the right. He squinted mysteriously.

Then, in a blur of motion, Waldo produced a hammer from somewhere and swung it with a vengeance. "Behold as this..."

Crunch!

The hammer smashed the amulet. Bilious blue smoke poured from the remains, stinkier than a sweaty warthog stuck in an elevator.

"Oops," said Waldo. He chuckled nervously. "Ur...smashing performance, eh?"

My two zombie captors let go. They blinked and looked about with wondering eyes. I sat up.

The bullhorn voice blared, "Come on out, Viesél. It's your last chance!"

Sammy and his dad looked at each other. The jig was up, and they knew it.

Mr. Viesél glowered at me. "You repulsive little lizard," he rumbled. "I'll have your hide."

"You wouldn't like it," I said. "It's too small to fit you."

Fweeeet!

Police whistles shrilled outside, ordering an attack. Two of Sammy's brothers tore into the room, all discombobulated. "Dad, the cops!" they shouted.

Mr. Viesél glanced at the hallway, then at the

window. With a frustrated snarl, he bolted for the back door, his family at his heels.

I strolled to the window and flung it open. "Thanks, coppers," I said, "you really saved my—"

Shock stole my voice like a bully pockets your lunch money. Nobody was surrounding the house. Nobody was blowing police whistles.

Nobody except a bigmouthed mockingbird.

"My pleasure," said Natalie. "Any time."

19

A Fair Shake

The flatfoots (that's what we detectives call the police) finally did show up. That night they nabbed the Viesél family trying to sneak out of town disguised as nuns. The weasels could cover their faces but they couldn't hide their bad habits.

My school seemed back to normal the next day (well, as normal as Emerson Hicky gets). During recess I met my client, Meena Moe, on the playground.

She smoothed her unruly hair. "Well, I suppose I owe you a debt of gratitude," she said.

"A few more quarters and some mosquito milk shakes would do the trick."

Meena rummaged in her book bag for coins.

With a shy glance from under long curly eyelashes, she pressed the quarters into my palm.

"You were so . . . forceful at the weasels' house," she said.

"Yeah, yeah," I said. "That's how us private eyes get the job done, with knuckles and know-how. Now, about those milk shakes?"

Meena rested a paw on my arm. My skin crawled. "I was thinking," she said, "that maybe we could meet at the ice-cream shop after school. Settle up my account . . ."

She gave me the flirty eyes again.

Sheesh. You do a dame a favor and she turns into a cootie factory.

I pulled my arm back. "Look, sister," I said, "just give the guy behind the counter a wad of cash and scram. I'll drink the shakes and let you know if there's any change."

Meena's buckteeth showed in a simpering smile. "Whatever you say, Chet."

I turned to leave.

"Wait," she said. "You're going, just like that? I haven't even thanked you properly."

Before she could come closer and lay a lip lock on me, I held up a palm.

"I'm going the way I always go, with a big smile and a quick wave, and the hope I won't be seeing you again anytime soon."

The memory of Meena's puzzled face made me chuckle through the rest of the day.

After school, Natalie met me at the ice-cream shop. We made sure that Meena was nowhere near, then we settled in and slurped our shakes.

"Ah, the sweet taste of victory," I said.

She toasted me with a frosty glass. "Here's chocolate in your eye."

Silence reigned until we'd finished our first milk shakes and started our second.

Then Natalie took the straw from her mouth long enough to ask, "So, what's the deal with those weasels, anyway? Why did they do it?"

I shrugged. "Love and money are the usual reasons. Mr. Viesél loved his work. And of course there's a lot of dough to be made from good kids' allowances."

Natalie snorted. "Yeah, like you'd know about that."

I let her wisecrack pass. I was feeling too good about myself, too good about the world. I'd pay her back tomorrow.

We slurped some more and watched the afternoon sun paint the trees with gold leaf. The next day, we'd have to start beating the bushes for another case. But first we'd savor the end of this one.

I belched gently. "Oh, man. I'm getting full."

"Me, too."

Then I heard the saddest sound in the world—a straw sucking air from the bottom of a glass. Natalie looked up from her empty tumbler.

"Should we have another shake?" she asked.

Our eyes met.

"Partner, we'd be fools not to."

Chet finds a mess of trouble
when he takes on
"The Hamster of the Baskervilles"

I raised my head and checked out my fourth-grade classroom.

Desks lay tumbled around the room like doll furniture in a cranky preschooler's playpen. Half-eaten papers covered the floor. Deep gashes raked the walls. A handful of seeds rested on the floor by the door. The seeds of destruction, maybe?

Most of my classmates stood gaping, saucer-eyed in amazement.

Bitty Chu tearfully fingered a wad of shredded paper. "Somebody's been munching on my math quiz."

Waldo the furball ran a finger along his toppled chair. "Somebody's been slobbering on my seat."

I noticed a jagged gash on the wall had mutilated my latest masterpiece, a safety poster. Somebody'd been slashing up my artwork—and I guessed it wasn't Goldilocks.

What twisted hoodlum could have done such things?

Mr. Ratnose stood knee-deep in the mess. His eyes were round as doughnuts, with a dollop of bitter chocolate in the middle. He sputtered like a deranged sprinkler head. Finally, he choked out, "Who . . . is . . . responsible . . . for this?"

Nobody moved, nobody spoke.

Bo Newt nudged me. "Whoever it was, he had monster feet," he whispered. "I'd hate to have to shop for his tennies."

I looked at the muddy footprints. Tony was right. Whoever made those tracks would wear shoes big enough to float downstream in.

"Who spoke?" said Mr. Ratnose. "Chet Gecko, was it you? Do you know something?"

For once, I passed up an easy target. "No, teacher."

Mr. Ratnose's whiskers quivered like an overstrung banjo. He paced up the aisle to me, wringing his paws. "You're some kind of detective," he muttered. "Can you find out who did this?"

I tilted my hat back and looked up at him. "I'm some kind of detective, all right—the kind that likes to get paid. If I track down this goon, what's in it for me? Can I get out of doing my science project?"

"No," said Mr. Ratnose.

"Can I get free lunches for a month?"

"Not likely," said Mr. Ratnose.

"Can I—"

"How about two get-out-of-detention-free cards and a box of jelly doughnuts?"

"Done," I said. "Mr. Ratnose, I'm your gecko."

**Look for more mysteries from the Tattered Casebook
of Chet Gecko in hardcover and paperback**

Case #1 *The Chameleon Wore Chartreuse*

Some cases start rough, some cases start easy. This one started with a dame. (That's what we private eyes call a girl.) She was cute and green and scaly. She looked like trouble and smelled like . . . grasshoppers.

Shirley Chameleon came to me when her little brother, Billy, turned up missing. (I suspect she also came to spread cooties, but that's another story.) She turned on the tears. She promised me some stinkbug pie. I said I'd find the brat.

But when his trail led to a certain stinky-breathed, bad-tempered, jumbo-sized Gila monster, I thought I'd bitten off more than I could chew. Worse, I had to chew fast: If I didn't find Billy in time, it would be bye-bye, stinkbug pie.

Case #2 *The Mystery of Mr. Nice*

How would you know if some criminal mastermind tried to impersonate your principal? My first clue: He was nice to me.

This fiend tried everything—flattery, friendship, food—but he still couldn't keep me off the case. Natalie and I followed a trail of clues as thin as the cheese on a cafeteria hamburger. And we found a ring of corruption that went from the janitor right up to Mr. Big.

In the nick of time, we rescued Principal Zero and busted up the PTA meeting, putting a stop to the evil genius. And what thanks did we get? Just the usual. A cold handshake.

But that's all in a day's work for a private eye.

Case #3 *Farewell, My Lunchbag*

If danger is my business, then dinner is my passion. I'll take any case if the pay is right. And what pay could be better than Mothloaf Surprise?

At least that's what I thought. But in this particular case I bit off more than I could chew.

Cafeteria lady Mrs. Bagoong hired me to track down whoever was stealing her food supplies. The long, slimy trail led too close to my own backyard for comfort.

And much, much too close to my old archenemy, Jimmy "King" Cobra. Without the help of Natalie Attired and our school janitor, Maureen DeBree, I would've been gecko sushi.

Case #6 *This Gum for Hire*

Never thought I'd see the day when one of my worst enemies would hire me for a case. Herman the Gila Monster was a sixth-grade hoodlum with a first-rate left hook. He told me someone was disappearing the football team, and he had to put a stop to it. *Big whoop*.

He told me he was being blamed for the kidnappings, and he had to clear his name. *Boo hoo*.

Then he said that I could either take the case and earn a nice reward, or have my face rearranged like a bargain-basement Picasso painted by a spastic chimp.

I took the case.

But before I could find the kidnapper, I had to go undercover. And that meant facing something that scared me worse than a chorus line of criminals in steel-toed boots: P.E. class.

Case #7 *The Malted Falcon*

It was tall, dark, and chocolatey—the stuff dreams are made of. It was a treat so titanic that nobody had been able to finish one single-handedly (or even single-mouthedly). It was the Malted Falcon.

How far would you go for the ultimate dessert? Somebody went too far, and that's where I came in.

The local sweets shop held a contest. The prize: a year's supply of free Malted Falcons. Some lucky kid scored the winning ticket. She brought it to school for show-and-tell.

But after she showed it, somebody swiped it. And no one would tell where it went.

Following a strong hunch and an even stronger sweet tooth, I tracked the ticket through a web of lies more tangled than a rattlesnake doing the rumba. But the time to claim the prize was fast approaching. Would the villain get the sweet treat—or his just desserts?

Case #8 *Trouble Is My Beeswax*

Okay, I confess. When test time rolls around, I'm as tempted as the next lizard to let my eyeballs do the walking . . . to my neighbor's paper.

But Mrs. Gecko didn't raise no cheaters. (Some language manglers, perhaps.) So when a routine investigation uncovered a test-cheating ring at Emerson Hicky, I gave myself a new case: Put the cheaters out of business.

Easier said than done. Those double-dealers were slicker than a frog's fanny and twice as slimy.

Oh, and there was one other small problem: The finger of suspicion pointed to two dames. The ringleader was either the glamorous Lacey Vail, or my own classmate Shirley Chameleon.

Sheesh. The only thing I hate worse than an empty Pill Bug Crunch wrapper is a case full of dizzy dames.

Case #9 *Give My Regrets to Broadway*

Some things you can't escape, however hard you try—like dentist appointments, visits with strange-smelling relatives, and being in the fourth-grade play. I had always left the acting to my smart-aleck pal, Natalie, but then one day it was my turn in the spotlight.

Stage fright? Me? You're talking about a gecko who has laughed at danger, chuckled at catastrophe, and sneezed at sinister plots.

I was terrified.

Not because of the acting, mind you. The script called for me to share a major lip-lock with Shirley Chameleon—Cootie Queen of the Universe!

And while I was trying to avoid that trap, a simple missing-persons case took a turn for the worse—right into the middle of my play. Would opening night spell curtains for my client? And more importantly, would someone invent a cure for cooties? But no matter— whatever happens, the sleuth must go on.